Elsa Beskow

# THE CHILDREN OF
# HAT COTTAGE

Floris Books

First published in Swedish in 1930 as *Hatt-stugan*
First published in English in 2012 by Floris Books
15 Harrison Gardens, Edinburgh
www.florisbooks.co.uk
© Bonnier Carlsen Bokförlag 2009
English version © Floris Books 2012
British Library CIP Data available
ISBN 978-086315-855-1
Printed in China

There was once a little man who lived in a mossy tree stump by a lake. He could mend shoes, make things out of wood, and he was very good at catching big fat trout from the lake. His tree-stump house was cosy and warm.

In the middle of the lake was a small island, where a little woman lived with her children. Sometimes she rowed across the lake to borrow a fishing net from the little man. Sometimes he made shoes from fine bark for her children.

The little woman and her three children lived in a little cottage. It was the shape of a hat! They called it Hat Cottage.

The children loved their little cottage and their mother kept it as clean as a king's castle.

One day, their mother said, "I have to go to the mainland to buy yarn to make you some new clothes. If you're good children while I'm gone, I'll make sweet honey cakes for tea."

The children loved sweet honey cakes. They promised to be good.

The little woman rowed to the mainland and knocked on the little man's door. "Can I buy some yarn from you?" she asked. "I'll take as much as you have. My children spend all day running and climbing and sliding and tumbling and their clothes are worn out."

"I'm sorry," said the little man, "but I don't have any yarn. Ask the spider next door."

But the spider said she needed all her silk. The little woman asked everyone, and no one had any wool.

At last she met a snail boy on the road. She had to bend down to hear his quiet voice. "Follow this path all the way to the swamp," he whispered, "and there you'll find more cotton than you can carry."

The little woman set off straight away. It was a long way to the swamp, but it was full of cottongrass with fluffy white heads of cotton.

Back at Hat Cottage, the children wondered what they should do until their mother came home.

"I know," said the oldest boy, "let's make Mother happy by sweeping the chimney. Just last night, some soot fell into her cooking pot. And it'll be great fun!"

They collected twigs to make brushes, and had a wonderful time climbing up and down inside the chimney, sweeping it clean.

The chimney was clean, but the children were not! They were covered in black soot from head to toe.

"Quick! We need to get clean before Mother comes home," said the girl. They took off their clothes and had a bath in the lake. Now they were clean, but their clothes were still as black as darkest night.

The girl thought for a moment. "Let's wash our clothes like Mother does on laundry day. Make a fire to heat the water. We can hang them in the sun to dry afterwards."

So they gathered lots of twigs and sticks and branches, big and small, and built a bright, roaring fire. They were having such fun that they didn't notice the flames getting higher and higher.

The little man had gone fishing in his boat. He was watching the fish dance in the clear water. Suddenly, he smelled smoke. He looked across the lake and saw a big fire on the island.

As fast as he could (which was quite fast, because he was a good rower), he rowed to the island.

The children saw him coming and hid behind a rock.

The big fire had already reached Hat Cottage. The little man threw water on the flames.

"Come on children," he shouted. "Don't be afraid! Help me bring more water."

The little man and the children filled his whole boat with water, and tipped it onto the fire. Smoke was swirling everywhere and they could hardly see Hat Cottage any more.

When the smoke cleared, Hat Cottage had disappeared. There were no walls, no door, no chairs and no roof. There was just the chimney and the cooking range left. Everything else had burned down.

The children cried and cried. Mother would be very very cross, and very very upset.

"You are naughty children," said the little man, "and this is your fault. But stop crying and I'll help you build a new house for your mother."

The children set to work collecting more twigs and sticks and branches, as well as birch bark, which is good for making a strong roof to keep out the rain.

The little man was very good at building and in no time, a new wooden cottage stood on the edge of the shore.

"We still don't have any clothes to wear," wailed the girl.

"We'll worry about that tomorrow," said the little man. "For now, it's getting dark and cold and it's time for bed."

He tucked them into their new bed and they fell fast asleep.

Soon, their mother came home with a boat full of cotton, enough to make lots of new clothes.

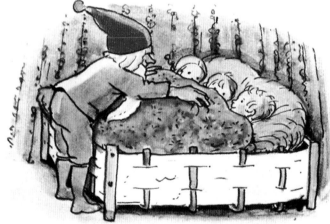

"Where is Hat Cottage?" she cried. "And why all the ashes? Oh dear! Tell me what happened."

The little man sat the little woman down gently, and told her the story.

"We've lost all our belongings," said the little woman. "I have no money and no one to help me. What shall I do?"

"Marry me!" said the little man. "I'll help you look after the children. We can live in my cosy tree stump in the winter, and here on the sunny island in the summer."

The little woman smiled, and said yes. And before long, they were married by Pastor Mole. The children had beautiful new clothes for the wedding.

The little woman and the little man were happy. The little woman sang merrily when she did the washing.

The children were happy too. And when they were good, they sometimes had sweet honey cakes to eat.